AF270211

German Shorthaired Pointers

by Grace Hansen

Abdo Kids Jumbo is an Imprint of Abdo Kids
abdobooks.com

abdobooks.com

Published by Abdo Kids, a division of ABDO, P.O. Box 398166, Minneapolis, Minnesota 55439.
Copyright © 2022 by Abdo Consulting Group, Inc. International copyrights reserved in all countries.
No part of this book may be reproduced in any form without written permission from the publisher.
Abdo Kids Jumbo™ is a trademark and logo of Abdo Kids.

Printed in China

052021

092021

THIS BOOK CONTAINS
RECYCLED MATERIALS

Photo Credits: AP Images, iStock, Shutterstock

Production Contributors: Teddy Borth, Jennie Forsberg, Grace Hansen
Design Contributors: Dorothy Toth, Pakou Moua

Library of Congress Control Number: 2020947580
Publisher's Cataloging-in-Publication Data

Names: Hansen, Grace, author.

Title: German shorthaired pointers / by Grace Hansen

Description: Minneapolis, Minnesota : Abdo Kids, 2022 | Series: Dogs | Includes online resources and
    index.

Identifiers: ISBN 9781098206024 (lib. bdg.) | ISBN 9781098206581 (ebook) | ISBN 9781098206864
    (Read-to-Me ebook)

Subjects: LCSH: German shorthaired pointers--Juvenile literature. | Hunting dogs--Juvenile literature. |
    Dogs--Juvenile literature. | Animal behavior--Juvenile literature.

Classification: DDC 599.772--dc23

Table of Contents

German Shorthaired Pointers

Both kind and smart, the German shorthaired pointer makes a great **companion**.

Breeders worked for years to create the perfect hunting dog. And they succeeded!

The German shorthaired pointer is named for where it was bred. "Shorthaired" is for the dog's short, thick, and tough coat. And the natural-born hunter stops and points when it finds its prey.

German shorthaireds are medium-sized dogs. They can grow up to 35 inches (89 cm) high. They can weigh up to 70 pounds (32 kg).

German shorthaireds can be
many colors, including black,
liver, white, and roan. They
have patchy markings.

Grooming

A German shorthaired's ears should be cleaned regularly. The dog only needs a bath every now and then.

Exercise

German shorthaireds need regular exercise. Hunting gives dogs plenty of work to do. Going on long runs and playing fetch are other good forms of exercise.

German shorthaireds are also great swimmers. Their webbed toes help them move in the water. They can either swim for fun or fetch downed ducks!

Personality

German shorthaireds learn quickly and are **eager** to please. Their **intelligence** needs to be matched with activity. This all-purpose hunting dog loves its family and a job to do!

More Facts

- German shorthaired pointers (GSPs) are good swimmers. They have webbed feet and strong, sleek bodies.

- GSPs can compete in and dominate almost any dog sport.

- While GSPs have short coats, they can shed a lot. Weekly brushing can help.

Glossary

bred – developed over time for a certain purpose.

breeder – one whose job it is to breed animals.

companion – one who spends time with another or others.

eager – wanting very much.

intelligence – the ability to learn or understand.

roan – having a dark coat thickly sprinkled with white.

thick – having parts that are very close together.

Index

Visit **abdokids.com** to access crafts, games, videos, and more!